Coffee & Explorers

By Irram Amin

*For my mother,
thank you for believing in me*

CONTENTS

Introduction……………… 7

Light……………………… 11

Darkness………………… 47

Spoken Word……………… 71

Short Stories……………… 99

Stage……………………. 176

Introduction

This is a small collection of poetry and stories written by myself. The poetry is raw and full of emotions, and will take you on a journey through my personal life. I have been through light and darkness, both closely and have created chapters dedicated to them. I have included many topics in these chapters such as, relationships, friends, death, family and religion. The third chapter, *Spoken Word,* is slightly less poetic and raw in emotion. It features my late father and in that, is where my emotions lie. The fourth chapter is called *Short Stories,* and is a collection of a stories I have written. They are not personal to me in terms of plot, but I take pride in them equally, as they are original pieces of writing. The final chapter is called *Stage.* It is the very first stage script

I have written and I am very proud to share it with you. Over the years, I have developed a strong bond with my family and an even stronger bond with my religion, Islam, so some religious tones are present in my writing. I have taken moments in my life that are very dear to me, and created this little book for you to enjoy. I would like the world to know that there is no shame in expressing your feelings, and I hope you enjoy reading my poems as much as I enjoyed writing them. And remember, the most magical and powerful weapon in the world, is your word.

Thank you,

Irram x

Light

She ordered a latte
with an extra shot of coffee
and sat down to write
the third chapter of her book.

I think she noticed me looking over,

You see, I had a thing for
coffee & explorers.

Magic lives there, she said.
In the littlest things,
that's why not everyone can see it
or feel it.

But she saw it,
and she felt it.

And she spread her wings
across the galaxy.

She made it.

And their souls harmonized,
like two perfect notes
in the symphony of life.

There was a time in her life
when she realised, she wasn't happy.

It was because she did not love
herself enough.

So, she decided to put herself first.

She put on her favourite shoes and
her favourite jacket and she was ready
to face the world.

She finally became the reason
for her own happiness.

She loved herself.

She faced her fears and she made it.

She became stronger and she made it.

She made it,

A thousand times over.

So many people are walking
past rainbows,
searching for a pot of gold.

Not realising, the actual treasure
is the rainbow itself.

Think.

Two opposite forms of nature
coming together to create a thing
of real beauty.

Do not ignore the colours of life
that are right in front of you.

Embrace them, enjoy them, and love them.

I apologise dear,
I sincerely apologise.

I tried to change myself
so you would accept me.

But I refuse to become *normal*.

How can I become grey
when my world is full of colour?

How can I become perfect
when my soul is full of chaos?

I love myself.

For the sake of love.

He put on his suit and tie,
and was ready to catch the lemons
that life was about to throw his way.

He was in a state of tranquil,
because when life was
kicking him down,
love was picking him up.

And it was
nature
that saved her,
from the wrath of
mankind.

The world does not owe you
a thing.

But you owe yourself
everything.

Every emotion and feeling
it takes,
for you to be happy.

Because you were the first one,
who your own heart
beat for.

And that itself,
is sacred.

Life means everything.

Yet sometimes,
it has no meaning.

Take me back in time where
life was simple and man was kind.

I want to camp under the stars
without the fear of murder or rape.

I want to throw Queen's heads' into
out dated vending machines and drink
a Kola without being judged.

I want to feel the wind in my hair
while I ride my bike.

I want to go back in time where no-one
judged you or hated you.

Where no-one was jealous of you or
ever haunted you.

I want to live in a world where

Life is simple and man is kind.

Your smile is the most precious thing you own.

It can be understood in every corner of the world.

Don't ever let its magic fade.

Your touch sent shivers
down my spine,

Yet you still managed
to set my soul on fire.

I wish I could live in my dreams,
because that's where all my
dreams come true.

There are books and
friendly robots,
rainbows and galaxies,
there is love and the smell
of sweet popcorn,
there are dragons and wildflowers,
there is colour and there is hope.

There is me, and there is you.

She loved the colour yellow,
sunflowers and lemon pie.
She was a fighter, you see
she fought the world,
and lived.

Fought her illness,
and lived.

Fought with fate,
and lived.

I called her my best friend,
and the world called her Kate.
Sadly, on a long August night,
she left this world to fly the
galaxies.

And as I lay sunflowers on her grave,
I realise she lives.
In my heart, and in yours.

I am an addict, I confess.
I crave the waves of
the ocean
and the leaves of an
autumn oak tree.

I feel a sense of enchantment
as I inject galaxies
in to my soul.

Don't just stand there,

Let's overdose on
wanderlust.

Sitting on a plane
doesn't teach you to fly

Sailing a boat
doesn't teach you to swim

A plane can crash
and a boat can sink.

But surviving?
You'll have to do that
by yourself.

Survival is created, and the magic
ingredient is you.

Trust yourself,
love yourself,
and find yourself.

I live for chaos

And for the

        Extraordinary.

She asked her mother,

> Why do people fall in love
> if it hurts so much?

My darling, if only you knew
how the thrill of such an
e l e c t r i f y i n g
pain numbs the soul. It's
extra-terrestrial.

Long distance love means
4am phone calls and looking
pretty for skype.

It means you travelling one
summer,
and me the next.

Long distance love has no
boundaries
because if you have given your
heart to one person,
then 7 billion others
can't get in your way.

You only have an
adequate amount of power to
change your own life

Do not depend on somebody else
to share it with
because in the end,
there will never be enough for you.

Sometimes, it doesn't have to make **sense**,

It just has to make you *happy*.

I believe in fairy tales
because they carry hope.

Not to be rescued by
fairy godmothers,
or swoon over knights in
shining armour

But to listen to your heart
when the world is against you

They carry hope that one day,
you can create your very own
happy ever after.

Graveyard visits are
perfectly entrancing

You know that you are
the only living soul around,

Yet you are standing over
millions of stories
waiting to be revived.

A bed of lies
concrete
blooming flowers
of truth,

Strongest muscle
tongue
power of nature
stronger.

You don't have to make it past
the finish line

You just have to make it past
the start line

Whatever happens in the
middle, is up to you
because only you have the power
to stop where you need to.

The sky moves
as the sea feels

The pen moves
as the mind heals

The wind moves
as the mountains kneel.

I cannot wait to show my children
the beauty of books and reading.
That beyond this world of misery
and chaos, there are other world's
they can find comfort in.

Even if it is for a brief moment,
it is always there.

I hope someone shows you
the light that was taken from me

And I hope that light burns
forever for you

I walk with prayer on my mind
and with hope in the darkest
depths of my soul.

He rose with the sun
and sang with the birds

Naked, wild and howling
for his mothers' milk

A most spectacular sight
a natural birth last night.

Try not to end your story
where it started

If the last chapter is the
same as the first,
your story will never be
remembered.

The world will give you happiness
but your Lord will give you
the world

All you have to do is ask with
your heart
           and
                  soul.
Praise Him

Acknowledge Him

Have faith in Him

Love me in the
golden hour
when the winds are calm
and the trees are calmer

When the leaves
change colour
and the f l o w e r s
glow brighter

When the air
grows soft
and the traffic gets
slower

And when the sunset has the urge
to ignite,

Keep holding me through this
golden light.

Darkness

You took my heart and soul,
the two things I hold dear

Now tell me, will you destroy them?
Because our love cannot
protect them anymore

You have two hearts beating for you
but yours will always be your own
and I fear for mine

Now tell me, will you crush it again?
Because I need it yet.

She was a nature kind of person
and loved long walks in the moonlight
with him
but one day he left her in the
middle of a forest
with nothing but the twilight sky
watching over her

She called for him and cried for him
she longed for him
she loved him
and she died for him.

And as her soul departed her body,
she saw him coming back
but not for her, no,
he had another victim on his arm.

He looked at her like maybe
she was magic

But she told him that
magic
      didn't
           exist.

I think he wanted me to
love him
but I couldn't

You see, I had loved
once before
and I had given him
all of it

So, I had nothing left
to give
but a smile and
my sorry eyes.

I wanted a fresh start
just me, in my own world.
I woke up one morning and
while I brushed my teeth,
I realised
that your taste was still in
my mouth
my gums started to bleed
but I could still taste you

It was at that moment,
I figured it wasn't just your taste
it was you
all of you.

You lived in my bloodstream.

The truth is
it was always going to hurt,

You just have to learn to
enjoy the pain

A broken soul
will teach you how.

They tell you that time is a
healer
and they tell you that you have
all the time in the world

But they do not tell you
the one thing we all fear

The fear of the end
$$\text{of}$$
$$\text{time}$$

The fear of *time running out.*

Of all the mistakes you made
I hope breaking my heart
was your favourite
because even though you pierced
it with the hottest needle,

It was done so swiftly
like a knight protecting his
queen

Thus, the sweetest pain I have felt.

The honesty of a man
leaves his body much earlier
than his soul

Much like a wilting rose
leaving behind sharp thorns
and colourless petals.

She wanted to find love
and be happy
but little did she know
to find love,
you must fall in to the
abyss of it and
learn to survive.

The day you died
my smile died too

When you left this world
my smile left with you

Now when I pray for your soul,
I pray for my smile too.

It wasn't just a loud noise
because I felt it
bouncing off my eardrums

Everything stopped
time froze for a moment
shards of broken windows
dug in to my chest
the airbag blew up in my face
I could hardly breathe.

Blood, sweat and tears
all mixed together
the sap of my soul

I care not for broken exhausts
for there is one regret I must carry
until my end

I should have died that day, not her.

Her soul danced with his demons
and sang the song of death
he had her soul in his hands
and she was helpless.

She saw her reflection in his eyes
and felt the fire burn within her
yet she did not feel guilt or remorse

Maybe her feelings had vanished,

Maybe,

She kissed the devil and liked it.

I was like you once,

Living,
      breathing,
             dancing
I was like you once
but I was killed
snatched from my mothers' arms
and shot in the head.

I was like you once
ate my supper on time
and went to bed on time
but then my house was destroyed
in a blast.
I survived. But they found me
snatched me from my mothers' arms
and shot me in the head.

I was like you once
but I pray you don't end up like me.

It was morphine I injected
to numb the pain
but the pain was mental,
                              emotional
It was incurable because your name
was engraved in every breath I took

Unless you suffocate my love
with the pillow we used to share.

Time doesn't wait for you
it runs from you
it didn't stop when my father
left this world and
it will not stop for your exit either

I always thought I had enough time
but it got away from me too
like dirty water racing through
the gutter
leaving behind distant memories
and my fathers' neglected gravestone.

Your artificial love
left me permanently masked
with synthetic feelings
and a manufactured smile

A theatrical mockery
then I guess,
the show must go on.

We hadn't spoken for two months
and so, I accepted my
paralytic state
sixty-two days of emptiness

Then, one night she messaged me
asking how I was

Remembrance can be a deadly thing
I felt my soul burn through my skin
tearing open freshly
sealed wounds

I was tortured by her existence
sixty-two days ago and
sixty-two days later.

You invaded our bodies
stole our trembling hearts
and like a thief,
escaped
forever,
from this world to the next

And now, this grave above the land
embodies a thousand hearts
beating in your memory.

I came home shouting
screaming, crying
ran upstairs and locked my
bedroom door
I put a pen to paper
my hands started to shake

You took away the only
cure for my emotions
the ability to write in
darkness

You've finally taken over
elected yourself as the new
president of my life

But you were always going to
win, because you had me by
your side.

Money. Fame. Greed.

And as he took his last breath,
he was surrounded by
everything he loved

But nothing that loved him back.

Loneliness isn't just
a feeling
it is a state

Which puts you in
a trance
and leaves you in a *state*.

Spoken Word

In the end, it **does** matter,
your colour, race and nationality.
Your status, looks and your personality
they tell you not to worry,
yet they take away your morality.
Well I'm telling you to worry, it's time
to face the facts here. It's time to face
your reality.
Your politics are sh*t and your government
is sh*t. You think they'll help you? Ha.
Joke's on you. They'll drop you six feet
under and tell the media you were a
threat to society.
They tell you money makes the world
go round, I say money makes the world
go wrong. You need to wake up, this isn't
a dream land. Basically, you need to fix up
on your distorted mentality.

A Cemetery Story

Mud on my shoes. I'm slipping,
tumbling over graves.
I clench the stems of white roses
tighter, as they lower him to the
ground.
Blood on my fingers,
forgot about the thorns. Sweet pain.
I whisper 'goodbye forever'
as tears reach my chin.
I wipe them. And repeat.
My vision is blurry,
I can't stop crying.
They had these flowers made for him.
Dad, brother, husband, son.
Even some in the shape of a car.
He loved cars.
All these relations lost; broken.
Time to cover him in a blanket of soil.
Inna Lillahi Wa Inna Ilayhi Raji'un.*
The cries are getting louder.
I place the roses on his grave.
It's over.
And I think to myself,

'All I have left of my father,
Are these next forty steps.'**

*Arabic phrase from the Quran – the Islamic holy book – and it translates to: 'To Allah we belong and to Allah we shall return'.
**In Islam, we Muslims believe that once a person is buried, their soul is questioned to start their journey into the afterlife. But this questioning only starts once everyone has walked forty steps away. The number forty is significant in Islam and is mentioned in many stories and of course, in the Quran.

We waste our energy on pain
and anger,
our time on crying and waiting.
We waste our years on lost souls
and dying emotions, and our
feelings on things that cannot feel.
If you woke up tomorrow morning
and the world was nothing but dust,
would you search among the rubble
for all the time that you had lost?

Remember when you were younger
and you wanted that chocolate from
the supermarket but your mother said no
because she only went for milk?
Remember the anger you felt and how
upset you were?
Maybe your mother had just enough for
milk that day and saying no to you
hurt her more than it hurt you.
For you, it was just another temporary
tantrum because the next time you ate chocolate,
you forgot about the supermarket episode.
But your mother will never forget
the pain she felt by not being able to
give you what you wanted.
A mother records every moment in your life
because you are her life.
Make them happy moments and give her
something to remember.

I speak for you
and I speak for me
I speak for right
and sometimes,
I speak for wrong.
I speak for the world to hear
and I speak for myself to hear.
I speak for passion
and I speak for insecurities.
I speak because I can
and I speak because I have to.
I speak for me
and you listen because you want to.

The truth is, you are scared.
Afraid of what has happened
and afraid of what may happen.
You feel like something is missing,
well that's because it is.
Whenever your heart broke,
you lost a piece of yourself.
Whenever you cried, you lost a piece.
And now, you are imperfect.
This is you now. Your broken pieces
are you. Your faults, weaknesses and
your insecurities, are all you.
So, gather all your pieces and present
them as yourself. Take pride in your flaws
and make your existence known.
Your beauty shines in ways you cannot
imagine. You are a work of art.
And art my dear, is *confident*.

I remember when you taught me
how to talk
and when you taught me how to walk.
I remember when you taught me
right from wrong
and when you taught me good from bad.
I remember when you would give in
to my every demand
and when you would cradle me to sleep.
I remember when your smile
started to fade
and when your heart started to break.
When he wasn't around anymore and
your memories started to erase.
I remember when you struggled for us,
when you cried for us,
when you gave up living your life for us.
I will always remember how you
gave your all to us.
Your strength is my confidence and
your confidence is my strength.

If he loved you, you shouldn't
have to question it at 3am.
Love is such a simple thing,
yet we humans make it impossible
for ourselves.
We dissect every feeling, every emotion
linked to love and in the end, we are left
with the remains of our animosity.
Love has such a sweet aroma,
yet we humans extract only the bitterness
from it and bathe in its' stench.
We are not satisfied with simplicity
so, we make it difficult for ourselves.
Then in difficulty, we search for ease.
We are a bizarre species,
'the human mind thinks but the heart feels'

And this is what makes me think, that the
symbol for love should be a brain,
not a heart
because lovers of today,
think more and feel less.

"My journey is a difficult one,
brown skin and a headscarf?
I'm asking for trouble."

You don't own me,
and you will never see me falling,
unless you're burying me
six feet under to my natural calling.
You tell me my attitude stinks
for a girl
and you think you can tell me
how it's supposed to smell;
let me tell you I'm proud of this aroma,
because it has traces of culture,
religion and my grandfather's
military personnel.
You're raising your eyebrows,
wondering who I'm talking about,
wondering who has the nerve to
question my character.
If you're raising them that high
and wondering that much, then it's you.
Yes you, sitting there, standing there
black or white, reading this in black and white.

The other side of loss

You left a hole, a void, a darkness.
Sorry, an absence of light,
an absence of you.
An absence that screams at me
every day and every night.
Remember, remember the 2nd December,
When I saw beyond the loss
and my soul danced to the
broken beats of my beaten heart.
The clock strikes 12. 12. I was only 12.
I remember, remember the hot flushes
as his body turned to ice.
I remember the rhythm of my heart
as his stopped beating. Don't die, don't die.
I remember the wetness in my eyes
as his closed forever.
The clock strikes 12.
Fast forward to now where
His voice is starting to fade
and his face is a distant memory.
But I've welcomed new love
and I've accepted new peace.
I've struggled to balance my cup of happiness

And now even though I'm in my 20s,
I'll always remember that a cup half full
Is also a cup half empty.
And as I've travelled through this journey
Of darkness and light,
As I've spent most of my life putting up a fight,
I finally listened to the voices that offered me help
Because in reality, I admit,
I had to lose myself, in order to find myself.

I mean, I still have trouble sleeping and I toss and I turn,

And believe me when I say, that my anxiety still gives me heartburn.

Don't get me wrong, I'm grateful for my life and I'm happy too,
But every time I smile or laugh, I feel guilty too.

Maybe this is who I am now – an organized chaotic mess…

But I know, that this is the start of my healing process.

The first six months

It was December that ignited the fire,
which still burns inside of me.
The month he was buried.

January. People are still praying
and I'm having endless nightmares.
It has only been a month without him
and mum had already started
to 'put his things away'.

It was February when we returned to school.
I remember everyone gawping at me -
Teachers and students all had the same thought
and everyone had the same thing to say,
"I can't imagine what you're going through".
At twelve, all I could do was smile and nod.

March wasn't any easier.
We were still making the mistake
of waiting for him to come home.
Still putting out six plates and six cups.
March was my parents'
fifteenth wedding anniversary.
We all muttered, "I love you"
but she longed for another voice.

By April, you'd think we'd slip into normality,
Get into a routine and 'move on'.
Truth is, we kept looking out the windows
and at the door.
Waiting for him to come home.
Home. It was just a house now, with four walls and
five burning hearts.

May. May. If I may.
Everyone else had returned to their normal lives
but we were still in limbo. Still lingering.
I started listening less at school and doodling more,
started sleeping less at night but dreaming more.

I turned thirteen on June 11th
and on June 15th, he would have turned thirty-six.
'Happy' birthday.
June fed my fire, making it impossible
for me to sleep at night. I thought I would
Choke from the smoke in my lungs.
But I guess, that was just the cigarettes.

The last six months

It was July when we realised how much
we needed school.
The summer holidays were *dragging* -
July felt longer than 31 days.
We needed sanity.

In August, mum took us away for a fortnight.
We spent four days in Egypt,
Staring at the peaks of Pyramids.
I love history.
Then we travelled to Mecca.
To pray for my dad.

September was exciting?
School had started again
and I was really looking forward to it.
But as soon as I stepped foot in the building,
the teachers and students had the same
Brief moment again, just a different question,
"How have you been coping?"
The question would hit me like a bullet.

When October came and
Nature was leaving us,
the nights got long

but mine, even longer.
The hands of time weighing me down.
A never ending cycle of darkness and pain.
Night fell, and I fell with it.

Remember, remember the 5th of November.
Every year he would spend hundreds on
Fireworks
and colour the sky for us.
But this year, we were peering
over other peoples'
Fences;
like stray cats and foxes.

So we've done a full circle
and we're back to December.
We're talking about death
anniversaries and
Visiting the graveyard.
I stood there in the mud,
thinking about all the promises
He didn't even know he'd break.
Then we came back to a cold,
empty house.

Roots & Stems

You say you support the cause

Because of the so called equality act,
But when it's free Palestine or Black Lives Matter
I see how you **don't** act.

See I'm bored of your questions
And I'm tired of answering them.
Do you drink?
Do you eat bacon?
Do you wear that thing to bed?
When you shower, does it stay on your head?

In a world where androids are kind of taking over,
Maybe the next time you say 'hey Alexa', you can finally find some closure.

I'm tired of spelling out my name to the Stephanie's
Siobhan's and Sinead's

If you can say **Dostoevsky**, then you can also
say my name.

I'm tired of being looked at in a different sort of
light,
And I felt it really deep when Maya said, "*Still, I
Rise*".

Brown eyes, green eyes, blue eyes,
All eyes staring as I walk down the street.
I wonder… what I've done wrong,
Or if I have something on my face.

Wait… I do.

I have culture on my face.
I have religion on my face.
I have the roots of my ancestors buried deep
within my soul.

YES! Look at me!

I am a walking, talking piece of art, heritage, and tradition.

I am the henna stain on Eid nights,
I am the colour of bazaars that shine bright
I am bangles, red, green, blue and yellow,
I am the street food at the end of corn fields,
I am the villages and the broken roads,
I am the sweet, ripe mangoes on a hot summer's day,
I am the smell of curry for breakfast on a Sunday morning.
I am spices. I am herbs.
I am garlic, turmeric, ginger, roots, I am strength.

I am Pakistani. And I am human.

And I come from all of this without being suppressed,
And I come from all of this without being oppressed.

In fact, I come from all of this this without violence and impurity,
Because my culture and my faith would never let me trade my humanity.

And my humanity stems from humble roots.

It stems from working class families and stay at home mums.
It stems from the death of my father and the sleepless nights of my mother.
It stems from you eating biryani and roast chicken while we had beans on toast.
It stems from choosing to pay for the bus or for lunch that day.
It stems from getting a job at 16 to help mum with all the bills she had to pay.
It stems from smiling on the outside while I was dying on the inside.

That's what kills.

I've laid out my timeline,

But it's not for you to judge,

I'm simply showing you what I come from,
And how hard I am to touch.

So, take me as I am, roots and all,
For it is not my fault if you stumble over them,
and fall.

Restore

Imagine looking at this planet from outer space

And seeing 7 billion bodies but not a single face -

Because were all taking different paths

At the speed of light

And no-one ever has the time to look up and say hi.

I mean, imagine being in a spaceship flying over the Earth

And seeing rich men making the poor one's work, while

The animals in the kingdom show mercy and equality.

I guess it's just us trying to rob the Earth of its tranquility.

It's not what it used to be though – a bright blue orb

Floating in the darkness with only the moon to guide its way.

Don't tell me it held on for so long

Only for us to take that away.

To strip it of its dignity and take away its tranquility.

Imagine if you were an alien

Looking down at us

And seeing spoilt little kids

Make the biggest fuss, over

Not having the latest phone or clothes to wear.

I mean, what does it matter if it's an apple or a pear?

And then you turn your head and see the other side –

The one that presidents and leaders try to hide

Along with the blood on their hands when they conquer and divide.

But what about all the people that have been cast aside

And when you start asking questions, apparently,

It's classified. Look at Yemen, look at Palestine.

And when you watch from above, its genocide. Magnified.

I just want to apologise for helping the Earth commit suicide.

Let's think about how the mountains are crying

And how the forests are dying,

How the people are lying about how hard they're trying?

And if you saw the Earth from up above,

You'd see neglected lands craving all types of love.

And listen,

We can change that; we can bring it back to life

With laughter and joy, and having God on our side.

We're merely travelling through this world

Trying to find our sanity.

So let's start by giving the Earth back its humanity and tranquility.

Short Stories

The Chair

"1889."

"I said 1889! Get up, time to go!"

"You didn't have to kick me", he muttered as he wiped the mixture of mud and saliva off his face.

"What did you say?!"

I was surprised at the volume of my voice in the tiny cell.

"Nothing officer".

Sometimes I forget that it's just a number and not his actual name.

"Miles, come on its time, I'm sorry", I couldn't believe the amount of remorse in my own voice. As he stood up – still shackled to the wall, a hot air balloon floats by; patterned with vertical shadowed lines. I notice his legs start to shake, like a newborn foal trying to walk across an icy lake. I shiver. I help him up by linking arms, unsure whether it was out of pity or just to get the job done quicker. A second officer comes in and releases him from the wall. The both of us exchange looks between one another,

"Let's go". My voice is surprisingly calm.

We get to the end of a long, damp corridor and are greeted with a third officer who is guarding a door which we need to get to the other side of. We hand him some paperwork and he unlocked it for us, the key to the door is an old rusted one, which screeches as it turns in the lock. The door swings open and there it is waiting for us, hungry, thirsty and vacant. The electric chair. Sitting in the middle of the room, a predator waiting for its prey; covered in purple and blue wires looking like bulging veins on a dying person. I could feel the chair staring at me, asking me to feed it and instantly, I felt numb. In my head I kept repeating '*Miles is a murderer; he killed his daughter and he deserves this*', so that I can sleep better at night.

Before I became a prison officer, I worked at a station filing cases and decided I needed a change; not realizing that it would torture me mentally and emotionally. The first time I stepped into the prison, I was petrified. You hear about all these riots that go on, and the number of officers that get killed (by being in the right place at the wrong time) with something like a melted down toothbrush. Imagine that, death by toothbrush. I was always on edge, not knowing who or what was lurking around every corner and I always felt like I couldn't breathe until lunch time or home time. But now, I'm used to it. It's like an automatic guard that's always up no matter what day or time; even on my days off, I'm cautious.

It was a particularly cold Sunday afternoon, considering it was the middle of July. The hairs on the back of my neck stood still the second I called out his number. I got out of bed that morning not knowing that in a few hours' time, I would be walking someone to their death. His name was Miles Scott, but we knew him as prisoner number 1889. All of our prisoners had 4-digit numbers assigned to them that often, some of the officers and I would often Google prisoners' numbers to see what happened in that specific year and Miles just happened to have the number that matched Hitler's birth year. *Freaky*. We have had Independence Day, world wars, you name it.

The details of Miles' crime were too much to

take in; the first time I read his statement, I was shaking, horrified at his words. (So maybe him having that number wasn't so freaky after all).

***

Miles was a devoted Christian (and reminded people of it) who went to church *every* Sunday, gave to the poor and carried the Bible around everywhere. He was a single dad looking after his daughter after his wife died of cancer. He was such a strict Christian, he always told his daughter, Lucy, to look for a **male** as her future spouse and to never have sex before marriage. Lucy was a 23-year-old student nurse who loved to party, stay out late and have a *normal* adult life. A life without the Bible, so to speak.

***

Miles was a paranoid dad (his words, not mine), he suspected Lucy had a boyfriend because of all the late nights, the dressing to impress and getting dropped off in a car with blacked out windows. He liked to keep tabs on her. Soon enough, his paranoia got out of hand so one day, he drove to her workplace and waited outside for her. While telling us all this, Miles had the same expression throughout. No remorse, no empathy. When Lucy had finished work, he followed her car and to his horror, ended up at an abortion clinic. He was *mortified* (apparently) and drove home in anger. When Lucy got home, Miles was waiting with his questions and asked her what had happened. Lucy broke down, tried to seek comfort from her dad and told him she was pregnant but did not want any children yet; so, she aborted.

This is the part in the statement where my stomach started to churn, the details are far too much for him *not* to be a psychopath.

"I went upstairs and called Lucy up after; I told her to sit down on a chair in my room, so she did. I had a rope, some scissors and a set of clippers under my blanket. As Lucy sat down on the damp wooden chair, I swooped the rope around her and tied her to the chair quicker than she could blink".

The level of detail was making me feel sick.

"I then told her she needed to be cleansed of her sins and picked up the scissors; I started to chop her beautiful golden locks. They fell so gracefully on the ground, like rays of sunshine lighting up the Earth".

This man was not normal.

Lucy was crying, she begged her dad to stop but he was too busy reciting verses from the Bible; then he picked up the clippers and began to shave. When he was done, everything was quiet, except he could hear birds singing and classical piano in his mind (of course he could the fucking *psycho*). This next bit is the worst, he smiled as he told us and paused for three whole minutes before he said it.

"I picked up the golden strands of hair off the floor and shoved them in Lucy's mouth, pushing down with more hair. Lucy was gagging, crying, and screaming. Dying. Oh, my dear, sweet Lucy."

He ended his statement with a smile, while exhaling a sigh of relief.

Lucy died of asphyxiation.

It was July 3rd and time for Miles to pay for his awful crime; although I think the electric chair was an easy way out for him and that too, the day before Independence Day? I think Miles had the last laugh. Free at last. The thing is, Miles would be dead in a while, and we'd have to pick up the pieces.

It was cold in the room, the chair was waiting for Miles' body to embrace it and melt in to it, like a lone candle, flickering in the wind. We unchained him, prisoner number 1889, and strapped his limp body to the chair. He had a smile on his face and was reciting something, he was muttering so I couldn't really make out what he said. I felt a chill and then suddenly, a hot flush. We had to step out and let the chair do the Lord's work; slowly, painfully. To me, it looked like the chair had the last laugh, an eye for an eye and all that.

Seyyal

2018

Seyyal Arvio was a very smart girl, she had knowledge of things you really didn't need to have knowledge of, like how a chef's hat has exactly one-hundred pleats or how the shortest war in history lasted for only thirty-eight minutes. She knew a lot of weird and wonderful facts, and she wasn't ashamed to show it. Seyyal was a daring seventeen-year-old, and came from a fairly big extended family, she was the youngest of three siblings and very spoilt. Seyyal was a short girl, slim but strong with piercing green eyes and jet black, straight hair. She had this beautiful smile, where her eyes would squint and smile too, mesmerizing you and leaving you in a trance. Seyyal had two sisters; Shayeen who was nineteen and lived in

Newcastle with her boyfriend; and Tania, who was twenty-two and working as a full-time nurse. Shayeen studied law at a university in Newcastle and often spent her holidays with her boyfriend's family. Seyyal didn't really speak to her sisters much, not even Tania who lived in the same house. She was either working, or out with friends and any spare time she had was spent on watching make-up tutorials on YouTube. Seyyal and her family lived in a four-bedroom house in Birmingham and she was in her second year at college, studying for her A-levels. She loved to read, anything and everything, and of course, the book was always better than the movie! It was the Christmas break and she was in the middle of writing her essay called *Poets on Opium*. She absolutely loved studying English literature, and hoped to become an author herself someday.

Just then, the front door knocked. At first, she ignored it thinking someone else is bound to be around to open it; when she heard,

"Seyyal? Sey? I know you're in there, please open the door!"

She started to shake hearing that voice. It was *him*. Baba.

~

Hakim Emraan was Seyyal's biological father but not to her two older sisters'. Their dad left Seyyal's mum, Bassima, while she was still pregnant with Shayeen. Hakim met Bassima at a local coffee shop where they had once been given each other's drinks by mistake. Love at first sight. They dated for a while and Hakim proposed within a month; and two months after that, they got married in a beautiful countryside manor. Hakim came from a very wealthy family and was an only child, and therefore, got everything served to him on a hot plate. He accepted Bassima's two young daughters and brought them up as his own. Hakim was a tall man, with broad shoulders and a chiseled jawline. He had a black moustache which curved perfectly above his top lip, and sleek, dark hair that had slivers of grey running throughout. He always wore a three-piece suit, no matter where he went or what he was doing.

"Baba? Is that you?"

"Yes baby it's me, please open the door."

"I can't baba, I'm sorry. You know I can't."

"Seyyal please, I'm your father, I'm begging you."

"Baba, you know why I cannot open that door.

Just go. Please."

"I understand, but can you please call me? You pick the time; I'll wait for your call. Love you."

Seyyal noticed a piece of paper at the bottom of the door with Hakim's name and number written on it. She hadn't seen her dad for over three years and she wasn't going to call him anytime soon. But three years ago, things were good, everyone was happy and Seyyal's family had it all. Love, money, friendship, respect. But all those good things came to an abrupt end.

Three years ago,

It was the morning before New Year's Eve and Seyyal was helping her mum prepare for their annual NYE party. Bassima Omar was a strong, confident woman, with an hourglass figure most women (and men) would *kill* for. She had sun kissed skin, big brown eyes with just enough kohl to make *anyone* swoon; and thick black hair that fell graciously just below her waistline.

"Sey, we need to make a shopping list for fridge stuff, I've got the freezer stuff ready, just the fridge stuff please."

Despite her inner battles and sleepless nights, Bassima took care of herself and looked well for her age, very well for her age, and she knew it. She loved the attention she would get when people asked, '*how* many kids?! And your youngest is seventeen?!' They would ask for her skincare routine and Bassima would just laugh and tell them that it was pure happiness and the love from her husband. What the people did not know was how untrue that was and how much effort and practice it took for her to keep up the

façade; and in her world, the show must go on.
"Alright its 11am now, I need everything done by 4pm, I'm going out for the evening."
"Oh? Where are you off to? Baba taking you out?"
"No your father's busy tonight, I'm just going out with some friends."
"Cool, have fun mum."

It was 5pm, Bassima had made dinner for the evening, everything was set for the party, and she got ready to go out. She wore a sequin black midi dress, strappy black sandals, and a red Ted Baker clutch bag matching her red lipstick. She curled her hair and looked at the mirror a final time before setting off. She dazzled. She walked down the stairs like a gentle summer breeze, and looked like a catwalk model. Hakim commented on her look and asked her where she was going. She told him she was out with some friends and not to wait up for her.

"Mum's said you're too busy to take her out so she's off with her friends instead."

Hakim looked at Bassima and raised an eyebrow.

"Did she now? But I kept tonight free."

Bassima started to worry and it showed on her face. She gave Hakim a dead look.

"Like I said, don't wait up."

And then slammed the door shut behind her. She got in to her car and lit a cigarette, started her car, and drove off.

~

Bassima walked in to a beautiful restaurant, it had a maroon carpet, draped tables, chandeliers, light music and an amazing bar. Bassima immediately felt relaxed. She stood around for a while until she spotted him by the bar. There he was, admiring her, smiling at her, taking notice of her. Her perfect man, her *secret* man. For a brief moment, Bassima felt a bit of guilt knowing that she left her husband and kids at home while she was out with another man, a total stranger to them; but then she remembered all the bruises and scarring Hakim had given her over the years and thought otherwise. She then walked up to her secret man and embraced him in a long, comforting hug. "Wow, you look beautiful." She smiled at him; she hadn't felt like this in years. They had a drink at the bar and were escorted to their table for dinner.

"I'm having a party tomorrow, for NYE, I want you to come."

Bassima stirred her cocktail and kept her gaze low.

"How can I come? All your family and friends will be there."

"So? I consider you closer, and it's not like you haven't been to mine before," she looked up at him and made eye contact. She looked sad, desperate, unloved.

"If you really want me there, I'll come."

"Thank you, there'll be so many people there you'll just disappear in to the crowd."

He took her hand into his, and kissed it. Bassima wanted to keep that moment forever.

~

It was 1pm when she woke up the next day. *Shit!* New Year's Eve! Bassima quickly put on her robe and ran downstairs. Seyyal and Hakim were watching TV – Harry Potter had been on every day and this was the sixth movie. Seyyal was a huge Harry Potter fan and was glued to the TV, even though she had seen every single movie and read all the books.

"Seyyal, will you help me honey? I need to call the caterers; will you start on the appetizers?" Hakim glared at Bassima and gave her a dirty look.

"It's not her fault you stayed out late and woke up at 1pm. Let her enjoy the movie."

Bassima didn't make eye contact with him and carried on stirring her coffee.

"Yeah whatever, I'll do it all myself."

By 6pm, everything was done, Bassima had

been working hard all day. The starters were done, the food was ready, the drinks were on the go, and it was a calm atmosphere. The guests were expected to arrive at 7:30pm but Bassima was anxious for one guest in particular. She went upstairs to get ready and Hakim was in their bedroom looking for a particular shirt.

"Have you seen my black satin shirt?"

Bassima looked in the wardrobe and around the room.

"No, I haven't seen that for a while. Check in the wardrobe but at the top where the old clothes are."

Hakim rummaged through the clothes and finally found his shirt; alongside something he wasn't supposed to find. Something secret, hidden among their items. Hakim froze. He then turned and continued to get ready. The mood was tense between the married couple but they were both ready to face their guests arm in arm and with a smile on their faces. Hakim wore a black satin shirt, black trousers and a pair of tan patent loafers. He looked handsome and ten years younger. Bassima wore a white silk gown up to her feet with embellishment around the neckline and sleeves, and had her hair in a low bun. They walked down the stairs together, in silence but arm in arm.

"Wow! Mum you look like an angel! The two of you look as if you're getting married again!" Seyyal laughed as she pointed at her mum's white gown and her dad's black suit. But Bassima and Hakim didn't find it amusing, not one bit.

"So Bassima, have you thought of any ways to kick Hakim out yet?"
Asked one of Bassima's closest friends, Yazmin. "I'll have him!" laughed another friend of hers, Layla, and they all drank and giggled at the silly idea of Hakim moving in with one of her friends. Yazmin was a tall, dark-haired and fairly slim woman and a single mother to two teenage boys. She believed that a woman can definitely survive without a man, but not the other way around. Layla, was younger than Bassima and Yazmin, around ten years younger, they met at a book club a few years back and the three of them became closer than ever over the years. Layla was a strong-minded, independent woman, who lived by herself in an apartment in the middle of the city. She loved to party and where there was Layla, there was always some sort of drama.

"No, I don't think I'll kick him out just yet. I like watching him struggle while I'm having fun."

She smirked at her friends as she pointed to a man standing by the drinks.

"Shut up! Who is that hunk?! Are you sleeping with him?" Layla whispered loud enough so both of her friends could hear.

"Maybe", Bassima laughed.

"So you're cheating on Hakim?"

"I wouldn't call it cheating if I'm only sleeping with one of them". Bassima smirked and this time, caught the attention of her mystery man.

"Bassima! You dark horse! He is such a hunk though, and he totally knows we're talking about him", Yazmin laughed, and finished off her drink in one big gulp.

"But isn't it a risk inviting him over to your

house with Hakim here?" Layla sounded worried for her friend.

"Not really, Hakim hardly notices what goes on around him, plus, it's a party! There are over a hundred people here." Bassima was slightly drunk and her words started to slur. She poured herself another drink from the bottle next to her and got up to dance.

It was 9:30pm and the house was full of guests, family and friends helping themselves to food and drinks, having a great time. Bassima was getting drunk by the minute and was slowly becoming a laughing stock. Hakim walked up to her and whispered something in her ear. She forced a laugh and followed him upstairs to their room.

"I need to ask you something."

"Hakim, what could be so important that you had to pull me away from our guests?!"

"It is important Bassima, it is bloody important!" Hakim was getting louder and louder.

"Hakim, what is it? You're scaring me."

Hakim sat down on the end of the bed and put his head in his hands. Before Bassima could speak, he got back up again and walked up to the wardrobe. He took out a white t-shirt and a pair of red boxers. Bassima went pale. At that moment, she would rather be anywhere else but there.

They weren't Hakim's.

"These are not mine. Who Bassima? Who? Are you cheating on me? Is there someone else?"

Bassima froze, she couldn't speak. She was

petrified. She didn't know whether Hakim was going to hit her or not, she was ready to flinch. She took a minute to think; *could this be a way out*?

"No. How can you say this to me? I'm not cheating on you!"

"Then what is this? These are not mine Bassima!"

Bassima started to sweat and felt a lump in her throat. She could feel the guilt start to mask her face when she thought of an excuse.

"No they're not yours. But I'm not cheating on you either. I didn't want to tell you before – well because I knew you would act like this – but they're Seyyal's."

"Seyyal? What do you mean they're *hers*?"

"Well, not her but she has a boyfriend and I found these in her room last week. I brought them here because I know the two of you like to watch movies in her room and I didn't want you to find anything and get angry with her. I'm sorry, I should have just told you."

"Really? And that's the truth? Are you sure?"

"Yes, Hakim. It's not Seyyal's fault. Please don't shout at her."

Hakim threw the clothes on the floor and left the room in a hurry.

Bassima sat on her bed and couldn't believe the lies that came out of her mouth. She started to cry in disbelief. Hakim would hurt her, but surely, he wouldn't hurt his only child?

She stood up to go back downstairs when she heard footsteps outside her bedroom door. The door swung open and there he was. Her mystery man, her savior in all of this.

"What are you doing here?! What if Hakim comes up?"

"He won't, not yet. I saw him leave the house in a hurry."

Bassima's mystery man went close to her and stroked her cheek. She held his arm and started to sob. He then embraced her in a tight hug, which felt warm. Bassima felt comfortable, like there was nothing in the world that could hurt her.

It was almost 11pm and the party was still in full force. Bassima's mystery man had left earlier because she told him it was too risky for him to stay. Hakim was upstairs in their bedroom; he had been drinking a lot and went to rest his head. Bassima sat with her daughters and smiled, she told them how much she loved them and they just gave her that look and thought, *you've clearly had too much to drink!* Bassima stared at Seyyal, her beautiful hair, her perfect smile and the thought of Hakim beating her black and blue. She couldn't believe the lie she had told about her precious daughter just to protect herself. She felt disgusted and ashamed and so, she went upstairs to confront Hakim.

Upstairs, Hakim was sitting on the edge of their bed with the shirt and boxers laid out in front of him on the floor. Bassima walked in and went straight up to him.
"Yes."
"Yes? Yes what?"
"I am cheating on you. I have someone else, because although I'm married to you, I am miserable! You don't love me, you beat me, and

you show me no affection!"

Hakim froze. He had a different type of rage in his eyes. The rage of a predator before biting into its prey. He was still sitting there, still staring at the clothes on the floor.

"Well? Say something!" Bassima was crying, purely because she knew what was about to happen. Hakim didn't speak. Instead, he picked up the metal photo frame from the bedside table next to him, and flung it at her. Before she could blink, Bassima was on the floor, shards of glass surrounded her head, her white dress slowly turning red, the embellishment turning shades of red and pink, and the cream carpet quickly staining. The white shirt that was on the floor, now had splashes of red across it; as if an artist had flicked red paint from a toothbrush. Hakim grunted, shut the bedroom door behind him, and went back downstairs. He poured himself a whiskey, knocked it back and went to find Seyyal amongst the drunk dancers.

"Seyyal, where is your mother? It's almost midnight and time to celebrate. Go and find her."

"Ugh Baba I'm with my friends, can't you go?"

"Seyyal, I'm not going to ask you again."

"Fine, she's probably gone to top up her lippy or something."

~

Seyyal's screams could be heard down the street. "SOMEONE CALL THE FUCKING POLICE!"
Oh my God mum. God please no, please no.
Seyyal found her mum in a pool of blood, her white dress stained red, her face slightly pale and her beautiful smile erased. Bassima was

rushed to the hospital in an ambulance shortly after and luckily, there was chance of her being saved. The doctor said she took a hard blow and lost a lot of blood, but it wasn't hard enough to cause her long-term damage. Bassima was in hospital for ten days after that, recovering and waiting on different test results. After being in and out of consciousness for six days, the girls finally heard their mum speak.

"Hakim? Where is Hakim?"

Seyyal and her sister Shayeen jumped from their chairs, and Seyyal started crying next to her mum. Shayeen had come home as soon as she had heard what happened to her mum.

"Baba left mum. He hasn't been home since the party."

"I see… he's run away."

"Run away? Where?"

"Girls, where is Tania?"

"She's at the house, there have been guests coming to ask for you and she has been tending to them. What do you mean he's run away?" Seyyal started to get anxious and teary. When her sister came and squeezed her hand.

"I think we should let mum rest and we can talk to her later Sey", Shayeen gestured to Seyyal that she should stop asking too many questions. Since she got back home, she has been suspicious of this whole thing. Where is Hakim? Why did he run away if he had nothing to hide?

"No, its fine, I can talk. I have to tell you something." Bassima got teary and her voice started to shake. The girls got worried and stood closer to their mum, each holding a hand.

"For the past three years, your father has been neglecting me, beating me, abusing me. So earlier this year, I met someone. Someone kinder, and loving and caring. We fell in love." Seyyal looked at her sister in shock, and Shayeen had an expression on her face as if she wasn't too surprised by this news.

"I was cheating on your father and was having an affair with another man. At my age, oh I'm so embarrassed." Bassima started to cry.

"There has been a man coming and asking for you at the house but we didn't know who he was so we didn't give him any information." Seyyal told Bassima he looked familiar but she was too scared for mum.

"If he comes again, be sure to tell him where I am."

"So, what happened with Baba after?" Shayeen was eager to know the truth.

"On New Year's Eve, during the party, your dad

found out and confronted me. At first, I lied and said it wasn't true and then I was thinking about it all evening and finally confessed. I thought if I confess, then I don't have to hide it any longer and I could have been saved from your dad quicker. Then, out of anger, he threw the frame at my head, like it was a known reflex to him. I have never seen rage like that before, ever. He left me for dead. I hope he never comes back."
Seyyal and Shayeen couldn't believe they hadn't noticed how Hakim acted towards their mum. Shayeen looked up at her mum and told her how sorry she was.
"He isn't coming back; we'll make sure of it." Seyyal stroked her mum's hair and smiled at her. "He's gone mum, and you deserve to be happy."

~

2018

Seyyal thought about calling her dad and she thought about forgiveness for a brief moment, but then she remembered the bloody dress, the stained carpet and her mum lying there, lifeless. *No way. He can rot in hell.* Seyyal vowed to call the police if Hakim ever came back. She started to type the rest of her essay but her hands were shaking and she couldn't stop thinking about his voice. The same voice that sang her lullabies when she was little, told her faraway stories and taught her to talk. *What if he was actually sorry? What if he regrets it? No. He nearly killed my mum! But she did cheat on him. What am I thinking?! That's no excuse to physically hurt someone.* All these thoughts were making Seyyal nervous, she felt sick. She loved her mum more than anything, but she also missed her father. She picked up the phone and dialed the number that was on the piece of paper.

"Hello?"

"Baba, it's me."

"Oh Seyyal, my beautiful girl. Thank you! Thank you for calling, you don't know what this means to me. Seyyal, listen to me very carefully, I need to see you. I'm innocent, and I can prove it to you. I did not hurt your mother that night all those years ago. Please meet me, so I can prove it to you."

Seyyal didn't know what to make of this.

"If that was true, why has it taken you all these years to make contact?"

"Seyyal, I wanted to make sure I had all the proof I needed before I came to you. Proving my innocence to you means everything to me. You are all I have. I had to make sure Sey, you have to believe me."

Seyyal thought about this for a moment. *What if he's telling the truth? After all, he is my father.*

"Alright then."

"Alright? You'll meet me?"

"Yes, I'll meet you. When and where?"

"Oh Seyyal! My beautiful daughter! Okay, listen, there is a café in the main shopping center called *Coffee and Explorers*. Meet me there for 2pm? I can send you the address if you like."

"No that's fine, I'll use the maps on my phone to help me."

"Okay. Thank you for believing in me Sey, love you."

"Bye Baba."

Seyyal put the phone down and realised how

much she missed her father. She needed this proof now more than ever.

Aliya

I sat in my car and watched from far as they lowered her body into the ground, while chanting their holy prayers. I wasn't allowed to her burial; her family had cut all ties with me because of our *haram* relationship. My Aliya was a beautiful brown skinned girl with fierce eyes and a smile that could melt butter. And then there is me, well I'm just a white boy from the estate. Our relationship was considered *forbidden,* as her mum called it. See, Aliya was a Muslim. And me? Well, I wasn't and that was the problem.

I could see waves of people paying respects to Aliya's mother, sister and brother. I could see the pain on her mother's face as she sobbed for her little girl. Aliya's coffin was in the ground now and I watched as they sealed her grave with huge slabs of cement. Soon after, her grave was a great big mountain of mud and flowers. Daughter, sister, friend, cousin. Different kinds of flowers decorated her lonely grave and my heart ached watching her life amount to nothing but mud, and flowers that are scheduled to die in a few weeks. *She must be so cold and alone down there.*

Aliya was my everything, the reason for my smile, my saviour and my best friend. We had plans to get married, move to Thailand, have a family and live happily ever after. But, sadly, that kind of stuff only happens in the movies.

Once everyone had left and there wasn't a car in sight, I put my key in ignition with shaky hands and drove it closer to her grave. Her *grave.* My lips quivered at the thought of her being under the ground I walk on. I looked around again and saw no-one. My heart started to beat faster as I got out of my car. I held a single red rose, and walked towards Aliya. My shoes were instantly covered in mud and I was slipping, tumbling over graves. I clenched the stem of the rose in case it fell out of my hand but forgot about the thorns. *Ouch!* As I approached Aliya's grave, I felt my body go weak. My legs started to tremble, while my eyes filled with tears. I knelt down beside her and sobbed as loud as my body let me. I couldn't believe I had lost the love of my life. I had so many things I wanted to say before I got here, but my mind suddenly went blank so I just sat and stared at all the flowers. It was the only grave with so much colour, which was a true reflection of my Aliya, always full of colour and laughter. I cried even louder thinking of all the memories we made together, and of all the memories we would have made in the future. My body was hurting from the pain I was feeling, nothing could replace the feeling of love, nor replace Aliya. I placed my rose at the head of her grave and left my last tears with her. It was time to say a final goodbye to the biggest piece of my heart. *I'll miss you. I love you.*

Nine days earlier

"Right, I'm going out for a fag Josh. You coming?"

Josh raised an eyebrow and looked up from his laptop,

"Again? You only went out half an hour ago!"

"Yeah I know but this is getting stressful now. I just need it to be perfect."

"Aliya, babe, it's only an open mic night. What's the worst that could happen? You go for your cigarette; I'll pass for now."

"Alright babes, won't be long." Aliya took out a single cigarette from her box, picked up her lighter and her jacket, and walked out of the university library. Outside, it was raining so she stood by the side of the building and lit her cigarette. She had her leather jacket draped over her shoulder. Well, it was Josh's jacket that she absolutely loved and 'borrowed' about four months ago. She wore dark blue skinny jeans, a black oversized sweat top and black chunky ankle boots. Her wardrobe was pretty simple and full of neutral colours which opposed her personality as Josh always told her, if she ever wore her personality as clothes, she'd be *full of colour*. She had beautiful brown hair that dropped gracefully just below her waist and brown eyes that sparkled whenever she smiled. She truly was a beauty.

Aliya stood under the smoking shelter listening to the rain pour, the water smacking against the plastic roof was helping her think. *It's not just an open mic night,* she thought. She was quite annoyed with Josh. She had worked so hard to get the University a spot at the spoken word event. Aliya finished her cigarette, squashed it with her foot and walked back towards the library. They were sat at the back on the sofas near the café, the smell of coffee surrounded them as they worked on the plan for the open mic event.

Aliya and Josh were both third year students at the University of Leeds and met at a party during their second year. They became really good friends and eventually, starting dating. For months, Aliya hid their relationship from her family because she came from a Pakistani Muslim background, while Josh was neither Pakistani, nor Muslim. She knew her mum would never approve, especially being a widow in the Pakistani community, because *people would talk.*

"I can't wait to graduate and get out of here."

Josh looked concerned. "Why? What's happened now?"

"Nothing's happened. I was just thinking while I was outside, I just can't wait for us to be together."

"We are together, Aliya."

"No I mean properly together, like living together and being a proper couple. I'm sick of hiding from everyone."

"Like your family?"

"Yeah. And from yours. Your dad isn't exactly fond of me either is he?"

Josh went quiet. Aliya was right, his dad was not fond of Aliya one bit. "Yeah you're right babe. We'll move away from everyone where it'll just be the two of us."

Aliya smiled and her eyes lit up. "Thailand still on the cards then?"

"Absolutely. The world is our oyster." Josh went to give her a hug.

"Stop! You're so mushy sometimes!"

"Yeah but you love it though." Josh looked into Aliya's eyes. "And I love you. You know that, don't you?"

Aliya smiled and nodded before kissing him on the cheek. "I love you too, mush ball. Now come on, let's finish this thing and get some food, I'm starving."

She moved closer to him and opened her notebook, "Look, you missed out this bit!"

Josh turned to look at her, "Babe, I'm sorry I have to head home after this. My dad's got his mates over and wants me home, you know how it is."

Aliya rolled her eyes. "Hmm, fine. Tomorrow then? Lunch?"

Josh grabbed her face and kissed her on the lips.

"It's a date".

It was getting late so the couple said their goodbyes and headed home. Aliya lived on the other side of Leeds so she walked towards the train station, while Josh drove home. They hardly travelled together because of the conflict between the two families; Josh's father Terry did not like Aliya while Aliya's brother Sameer, did not like Josh. Their reasons were the same – Josh and Aliya should be with someone from the same race.

***

Aliya stood on the platform waiting for her train to arrive. She untangled her earphones ready for the journey ahead. Her hands were freezing and she couldn't quite get that final knot which frustrated her, so she used her teeth instead and managed to untangle them completely. *The 19:14 train to Leeds central station is arriving on platform three. Please mind the gap.* The train finally arrived and Aliya boarded it. She found two empty seats – one for her and the other for her bag, at least until someone else comes who needs the empty seat. Luckily, no one did.

Aliya's mum picked her up from the station.

"How was your day puttar?"

Aliya shrugged her shoulders,

"Yeah it was alright".

She hated it when her mum called her *puttar*. It reminded her of her roots, which she despised, since her family made their feelings clear about Josh. Her mum's tone changed.

"You stink of smoke, it's disgusting."

Aliya looked towards her mum,

"It wasn't disgusting when you were doing it, was it?"

There was silence after that. Both Aliya and her mum remained silent for the whole journey home. Aliya can always tell when her mum is annoyed with her. She starts to get angry at the other drivers for no reason and her gear shifting gets aggressive by the minute. Aliya looks out of the window and sighs.

***

By the time Josh got home, his dad, Terry, was already on his third beer can.

"Where have you been then? With that p*ki of yours again?"

Josh looked at his dad, he could feel the rage climb his body through the pit of his stomach. He wanted to say something, to shout at his father and tell him exactly what he thinks. But he couldn't. And Terry knew that.

Terry sneered at his son. He was a tall man with broad shoulders, blue eyes and no hair. He always wore blue jeans with some sort of t-shirt that sat snug around his beer belly. He was a plumber by day and an alcoholic by night. Josh was Terry's only child and he raised him all alone after his wife left him for another man.

"Where you going Joshy?"

Josh glared at his father, who had a smug look on his face.

"Upstairs. I have some work to do."

Terry attempted to stand up, swaying, when he flopped back onto the sofa.

"Leave it for tonight, my mates are coming over and they want to talk to you."

Josh looked worried.

"Why do they want to speak to me?"

Terry smiled.

"Oh you know. Just guy talk. Besides, they haven't seen you for a while now. Probably because you're always out with that pa-".

"With who?! Go on, say it then!" Josh interrupted his father, his voice echoing around the house. Terry chuckled and looked away.

Just then, the door knocked and Josh walked over to open it. It was Terry's two friends, Paul and Tom, each of them holding a six-pack of beer. "Alright Josh! How you doing mate?" Tom was loud, and shared Terry's confidence, while Paul was quiet. They didn't wait for a response from Josh and walked in. They went straight to the fridge, swapped their beers for colder ones and walked over to greet Terry.

"Come on Josh!" Shouted Terry from the far end of the living room.

Josh couldn't understand why his dad desperately wanted him there. His mates always come round, so, what was so special about today?

"Dad, I told you, I have work to do. What's so important anyway?"

Josh was getting nervous; his palms were starting to sweat. He didn't really like Tom or Paul, they were very expressive about their views – especially views on people who were not white. Josh couldn't bear being around them and he could feel the heat from the three men around him, but, for his dad's sake, he stayed.

"Fine, I guess my work can wait until tomorrow."

Terry was made up. His smile stretched so far, you'd think his lips would crack.

"That's more like it! Go and grab yourself a beer."

Josh felt nervous drinking around his dad and his friends.

"Just the one then."

Terry's friend Tom was the alpha male of the group, he knew his stuff and he knew when to work a person. Tom came from a well-educated background; he was previously a secondary school teacher; back when he was a closet racist. After 'coming out', he was fired from his job as a teacher and decided to embark on his journey of *'sending immigrants where they came from'*. Tom wasn't afraid to speak his mind, even if it meant he was spewing hate. He was an average height with heavy tattoos and only wore designer clothes. A pompous fool, according to Josh.

"So Josh, you dumped that girlfriend of yours yet?"

Paul looked up at Tom, who had a smug look on his face while he waited for Josh to answer. Paul was a lot younger than Terry and Tom and met them when he was in sixth form at the school Tom taught at. He became good friends with Tom and believes Tom showed him the way of life. The school backed off as soon as he turned eighteen and Tom had complete control over him. Josh was aware of this and that is one of the many reasons he doesn't like being around them, not for too long.

Josh looked over at Tom.

"No I haven't. And I'm not going to either."

Terry started to look uncomfortable, it was clear that he was afraid of Tom. He chuckled nervously,

"Well… he's going to soon, aren't you son? I mean it's never going to last is it? You, a white lad with, *her.*"

Tom smirked and looked over towards Paul who tried to hide his laughter. Josh was furious. He could feel the beer can slip from his palm because of the sweat.

"Shut up dad. Shut up! All of you, just shut up! Aliya is my girlfriend and one day I'm going to marry her. Just piss off you racist pigs!"

He stood up and looked Tom in the eyes.

"I'm getting out of here, I don't need your shit views or your shit company."

He slammed his can on the table and walked out of the house slamming the door behind him. The three men looked at one another until Tom took a big gulp of his beer and chuckled to himself.

"He'll come around. They always do, don't they Paul?"

Paul glanced over at Terry with a nervous look in his eyes.

"Erm yeah course mate. Don't worry."

Tom sat up and placed his can on the table.

"Look, Terry mate, what do you want to do? Or better even, what will you have *us* do?"

Terry knew his friends meant business and he was in it for the long haul.

"Do whatever you think necessary Tom, I just want my son back. He's all I have."

The next morning, Aliya was waiting on the platform for her train to university. She had her earphones in and was listening to an audio version of *Pride and Prejudice*. She wasn't a fan of *Jane Austen* but it was one of the books she had to study for her literature module. The train arrived and Aliya boarded it. She found an available seat but this time, someone came and sat next to her so she had to hold her bag in her lap. Luckily, she got the window seat. A man with a brown leather jacket, blue jeans and converse trainers came and sat next to her. Aliya looked at him and gave a friendly smile. It was Tom, Terry's friend. The train started to move and Aliya tried to get comfortable. Tom tapped Aliya on the shoulder. She took out her right earphone with a confused look on her face.

"Hi, can I help you?"

She looked at him up and down, trying hard to think if she knew him from anywhere.

"Are you Aliya?"

She froze.

"Er… yes. Do I know you?"

Aliya felt uncomfortable. She did not know this man and yet, he knew her.

"My name's Tom, I'm a friend of Terry's. Josh's dad?"

Tom smiled at her but Aliya knew that smile meant something else. A friend of Terry's meant trouble and nothing more.

"Look Aliya, I'm here as a friend. To kindly ask you to leave Josh, it's in everyone's best interests."

Tom put his hand on her leg.

"Do we understand each other?"

Aliya pushed his hand off her leg and gave him a stern look.

"No we don't. I don't know who you are and quite frankly, I don't care. My relationship doesn't concern you, so, if you don't mind, I'd like to leave."

Tom smirked and turned his body towards her.

"Aliya, don't make this difficult. Josh isn't good for you. He's not even a Muslim like you. You sure your family will accept a white boy?"

Aliya realised what this was all about. Of course, how could it be about anything else? After all, he was a friend of Terry's, who hated Aliya simply because she wasn't white.

"Like I said, my relationship is none of your business so, if you don't mind, I'd like to leave."

Tom smiled and pivoted around to let her out.

"See you around, Aliya."

Aliya walked down the aisle of the train carriage and towards the doors. The train nearly came to a stop and she was getting ready to get off. Her heart was pounding so much and she was standing so close to the door that if they suddenly opened, she would have definitely fallen through. Once she got off the train, she looked back to see if she was being followed but there was no one there. She clutched her bag close to her and searched for her phone. She tried calling Josh but there was no answer. She started to worry and random thoughts started to occupy her mind. *Why isn't Josh picking up? Where is he?*

It had been two hours since Aliya called Josh and there was still no response from him. She called him once more and still, no answer. About half an hour later, she received a text from him, which read:

```
Aliya. I'm really sorry.
I can't do this anymore.
I'm breaking up with you.
My dad's right, this is never
going to work... we don't
really have a future together.
I'm so sorry. Love you always, J x
```

Aliya was mortified. She felt her neck heat up while her jaw started to clench. Her whole world had come crashing down in a flash. She looked around and in an instant, felt alone. *How can Josh just break up with her? This was unlike him.* Aliya tried to call him again but this time, it went straight to voicemail. Her eyes widened and she stood still, as if time had frozen for her. She started to panic and rushed outside for some fresh air. Aliya stood outside the building with her phone clenched in her hands. She took out a cigarette from her bag and lit it. After a huge puff, she sighed. She read the text again. And another four times after that. This was unlike Josh, he would never do this to her, especially without a reason. What was she supposed to do now? How can she go home and tell her family? She had argued with her mum just last night about her relationship with Josh. What was she supposed to say now? Aliya was distraught. Her world of colour had instantly been drained. She was so confused and tried to think of every logical reason as to why he would do this to her. Maybe Terry was putting pressure on him. Or maybe that Tom guy was behind all of it. She tried calling him again. Voicemail, again. Aliya started to cry. She wanted to run away and never come back. She felt like without Josh, she had no one. Aliya felt like she had nothing to live for without him. It was over. She walked back inside the university building and walked straight past her next lecture room. She walked so fast and ended up outside the cleaning cupboard. Aliya remembered Tom's smug face. She remembered her mum's harsh words and she remembered Josh's text. He dumped her over a text message. Tears were streaming down her face, her ears were burning from the stress and in that moment, she made her choice. She opened the cupboard and walked in. She looked around the shelves and saw a bottle of bleach. She was sobbing so much, her head started to hurt. She turned the cap and the whiff of strong bleach made her gag. She put the bottle down and took out her phone from her pocket. She called Josh one more time. *Welcome to the o2 messaging service, the person you are calling is unable to take your call.* Voicemail, again. Aliya picked up the bottle and took a big sip. She struggled to swallow it at first and then, felt the burning sensation as it travelled down her body.

Terry was in his bedroom with the door locked.

"Dad! Open your door! And give me back my fucking phone. I'm not a kid, what are you playing at?"

Terry waited a while and thought about it for a moment. He realised that he is losing his son either way, so he walked over and opened the door. He handed Josh his phone back.

"I'm sorry son."

Josh snatched the phone out of his dad's hand and walked off without saying a word. When he got to his room, he sat on his bed with a huge sigh. He switched his phone on and saw three texts from his friends asking where he is and one text from Aliya. At first, Josh was confused at the text message until he read the one above it. It was from him, but he didn't type it. He rushed back to his dad's room to confront him.

"Dad what the fuck are you playing at? You text Aliya telling her I broke up with her?"

Terry looked guilty.

"I'm so sorry son, it was all Tom's idea."

Josh was filling with anger.

"Tom?! Ugh just leave it dad!"

He rushed downstairs and grabbed his car keys. He drove to the university to look for Aliya. On his way, there was a lot of traffic and he realised it was because everyone was giving way to a police car and an ambulance coming from the opposite direction. After parking his car, he ran towards the entrance. He ran straight into the lecture room that Aliya was supposed to be in and saw it was empty. He turned and ran to the information desk to enquire about Aliya's lecture. He was panting and sweating. A bad feeling ran through his body.

"I'm sorry Josh," the lady at the desk looked distraught.

"Aliya's gone."

Josh felt his body turning to ice.

"Gone? What do you mean gone? Gone where?"

The lady at the desk looked at him with sorry eyes.

"Aliya was confirmed dead and taken in an ambulance not long ago. They think she drank something from the cleaning cupboard. I'm so sorry."

Confirmed dead? My Aliya? Josh vision went blurry and my ears started to ring. My chest started to feel tight and I felt like I was drowning. My Aliya was confirmed dead? She died thinking she was all alone. I screamed so loud I felt the world around me come to a standstill.

Stage

Morning Prayer

by Irram Amin

A Stage Script

Character list

Sabir – a sixty-five-year-old widower

Maria – Sabir's eldest grandchild, lives with Sabir

Zara – Maria's younger sister, lives with Sabir

Kidnapper – familiar to Sabir

Scene 1   Sabir's house - Birmingham, England, 2015

Inside SABIR'S bedroom, USR. It is the middle of the night. SABIR is sleeping on a double bed which has a bedside table to the right of it. On the table, is a white lamp, a pair of reading glasses and a copy of the Qur'an. SABIR is having a nightmare which eventually wakes him. He can hear the clock ticking over his heavy breathing. His screaming had also woken up his two grandchildren who sleep in the room next to his.

SABIR: Please God, forgive me.

(SABIR is sweating and praying)

SABIR: Astaghfirullah. Astaghfirullah. Astaghfirullah.

(The grandchildren enter SABIR'S room, SR. ZARA switches on the light and they see SABIR crying and praying, frantically)

ZARA: Grandad!

MARIA: Quick! Get him some water.

(MARIA helps SABIR to sit up while she props a cushion behind him. ZARA walks over to a chest of drawers and picks up a bottle of water, DSR. She hands the bottle to SABIR. MARIA puts her hand on SABIR'S shoulder and gives him a comforting look. SABIR holds MARIA'S hand and squeezes it)

MARIA: Grandad? It happened again didn't it?

ZARA: What? What happened?

(SABIR and MARIA exchange looks. SABIR puts the water bottle on the floor and turns to ZARA)

SABIR: I've been having the same nightmare for a week.

ZARA: (looking at MARIA) And you knew about this?

MARIA: Well, I-

ZARA:	I can't believe this. Grandad has been suffering for a week and you didn't think to say anything?!
SABIR:	I wouldn't exactly call it suffering Zara. I think you're over-reacting a bit.
ZARA:	Over-reacting? But I'm worried about you. What was the nightmare about anyway?
MARIA:	I think we should leave him alone and let him sleep.
ZARA:	Oh, so it's alright for you to know about it but not me?
MARIA:	I didn't say that. I just don't want to upset grandad.
ZARA:	Of course, the favourite grandchild gets to know it all.

(ZARA gets up to leave)

MARIA:	Zara listen-
ZARA:	No. Not to you.
MARIA:	Why are you so offended?

SABIR: Girls, stop. Wait there Zara.

(SABIR looks over to MARIA)

SABIR: It looks like we're wide awake now anyway. So, what harm will it do to talk about it?

MARIA: But grandad, I don't want you having another nightmare by talking about it.

SABIR: (sighs) I've lived the real thing. Come on Zara, sit down.

(ZARA walks over to the bed and sits down next to her sister)

ZARA: I still don't understand. Are you talking about the kidnapping?

(SABIR nods)

ZARA: But I already know about that. Mum told me.

MARIA: Did she tell you everything? Even about the cave?

ZARA: Cave? What cave?

SABIR: (sighs) What exactly did your mother tell you Zara?

ZARA: Mum said that you got taken by these bad men and you managed to escape.

SABIR: But she didn't give you the details?

ZARA: Not really.

SABIR: Alright tell you what, why don't you go and make us some tea? And when you come back, I will tell you about the cave.

(ZARA looked over at MARIA)

ZARA: Do you want one too?

MARIA: Want what?

ZARA: (rolling her eyes) Tea?

MARIA: Oh yeah, sorry. Yes, please.

ZARA: (getting up from the bed) Cool, be right back.

SABIR: And don't forget my saucer!

ZARA: (laughing) I know grandad!

(ZARA exits, SR. SABIR looks over at MARIA while he fixes the bed sheets)

SABIR: Maria, what's wrong?

MARIA: Nothing, why?

SABIR: Then why do you look so sad?

MARIA: I just hate the thought of you being in that cave all alone.

SABIR: (smiles) But I wasn't alone. I had Allah by my side.

(MARIA smiles back at SABIR. She stands up, walks over to him and gives him a hug)

MARIA: Do you ever miss it?

SABIR: What, Pakistan?

MARIA: Yeah, do you miss it?

SABIR: Of course I do, it's my homeland. *Our* homeland. But since your Nan died, it hasn't really felt like home.

(MARIA notices SABIR'S eyes starting to tear up)

SABIR: But I am grateful though, I have my family around me and Allah has blessed me with a second chance at life. You know Maria, you shouldn't be so harsh on your sister. She's only trying to be like you.

MARIA: Be like me? I don't think so. Zara is her own person and no force of nature can change that!

(MARIA and SABIR laugh. ZARA enters carrying a tray with three cups of tea, SR)

ZARA: Talking about me?

MARIA: (looks at ZARA and smiles) Always.

(ZARA hands the teas out, takes one for herself and sits down beside her sister)

ZARA: Come on then grandad, let's hear it. What's all this about a cave?

SABIR: It was my closest encounter with Allah.

ZARA: What do you mean?

SABIR: Look Zara, when you are in trouble or when you are scared, what do you do?

ZARA: I pray.

SABIR: And do you believe your prayers will work?

ZARA: Sometimes.

SABIR: Well, that night, 'sometimes' wasn't enough for me. It HAD to work because it was my only option.

ZARA: What do you mean it *had* to work?

SABIR: That night, my prayers saved me. Allah gave me the power to survive.

(SABIR puts his cup down and faces the two girls)

SABIR: That night felt like the longest night ever. I feared for my life. It was after two of the kidnappers had left to find food. I was in a cave while the third kidnapper stood guard. I was sitting on the cold hard floor and felt so weak. I could feel my body giving up on me. I tried to look for ways to escape, but it was so dark I could hardly see.

(Lights go dim, exit all characters)

Scene 2   The Cave – Pakistan, 2004

SABIR is sitting on the cave floor while the KIDNAPPER is standing guard outside, CS. The cave is dark and is surrounded by brambles and nettles. The floor is covered in rocks and sand.

SABIR peers towards the KIDNAPPER. He is weak and limp after being dragged across fields barefoot. His clothes are torn and his feet are bloody. SABIR brushes dust off his face and looks around for an opening in the cave. SOUND EFFECTS – wind blowing, rocks and pebbles scattering

The KIDNAPPER is pacing up and down outside the cave, his face is covered with a scarf. SABIR crawls towards the KIDNAPPER.

SABIR: (wearily) Please, tell me where you are taking me.

(The KIDNAPPER looks in SABIR's direction but does not speak)

SABIR: I beg you, I'm an old man, have mercy.

KIDNAPPER: Stop talking!

SABIR: (whimpering) Are you going to kill me?

KIDNAPPER: I will if you don't stop talking!

(SABIR crawls closer and notices the KIDNAPPER is unarmed)

SABIR: (to himself) Do I have a chance? Allah give me a sign, please.

(SABIR puts his hands together and starts to pray)

SABIR: Oh Allah! Please help me, I am a slave of yours. Oh Allah! Protect my children. Help me out of this misfortune, have mercy on me.

SABIR sat with his back against the cave wall and prayed to Allah. He picked up some small stones and used them as prayer beads. His eyes had finally adjusted to the dark so he stood up, walked around the cave trying to find an opening. He was desperate to escape and save himself.

KIDNAPPER: Hey! What are you doing? Sit down and don't make a sound!

SABIR: My legs are stiff from sitting down, I was just trying to move them

KIDNAPPER: Well, don't.

SABIR: Will you tell me your name?

KIDNAPPER: (sneering) Do you think I'm stupid? I'm not going to ask you again to be quiet.

(The sun began to rise – low light emerging from SR)

SABIR noticed it getting lighter, he realised it was time for morning prayer. He approached the KIDNAPPER

SABIR:	Excuse me brother?
KIDNAPPER:	I'm not your brother. Didn't I ask you to stop talking?
SABIR:	Yes, I know, but this is important.
KIDNAPPER:	What is it?
SABIR:	It is time for morning prayers, please allow me to pray.
KIDNAPPER:	You can pray in the cave.
SABIR:	What's the harm in me coming out to pray? You'll be watching me anyway.
KIDNAPPER:	(hesitantly) Alright fine. But here, where I can see you.

(SABIR walked out of the cave and performed the act of wudhu using sand. He then began his prayer, SR)

SABIR: Allahuakbar. Allahuakbar.

(SABIR sat on the floor with his hands on his knees while he prayed)

SABIR'S prayer came to an end.

SABIR: Assalaamualaikum
                      Warahmatallah,
                      Assalaamualaikum
                      Warahmatallah.

SABIR looked at both shoulders as he finished his prayer and just as he turned to his left shoulder, he noticed something in the distance. SABIR spotted a light coming from the back of the tunnel. He looked at the KIDNAPPER who wasn't paying much attention and thought about his escape. He raised his hands for one last prayer and gathered all his courage. SABIR stood up. And he ran. He ran towards the light and he didn't stop to look back.

Lights go dim – exit all characters

Scene 3   Sabir's house - Birmingham, England, 2015

Back in Sabir's room, ZARA has tears running down her face while MARIA holds SABIR's hand.

ZARA: What happened after that? Did he not chase you?

SABIR: Oh yes, he did. But I was determined to outrun him.

MARIA: There's one thing I don't understand though.

SABIR: What's that?

MARIA: You said you felt weak when you were in the cave. So, how did you run so fast?

SABIR: (smiling) I told you, I prayed. I believe Allah gave me the strength I needed in that moment. That's why I've been even closer to faith ever since.

ZARA: Wow. So, I'm guessing he never caught you?

SABIR: Wrong. He did catch up to me.

ZARA: What? How? What happened?

SABIR: (looking at Maria) We fought.

ZARA: Why are you looking at her like that?

SABIR: Well, it got messy.

ZARA: (nervously) How… messy?

SABIR: I was running barefoot through a field full of nettles, stones and all sorts. Plus, now that the sun was out, he could see exactly where I was. I kept running until I saw a ditch and had no other option but to jump and hope for the best.

ZARA: Whoa. This should be a book.

MARIA: Shut up Zara, don't be so disrespectful.

ZARA: Sorry.

SABIR: It's alright, it does sound like quite the action movie.

ZARA: So, what happened after you jumped?

SABIR: I landed in some nettles and thorns

ZARA: Ouch! What about the man?

SABIR: He jumped in after me. He wasn't ready to give up. He started to wrestle with me

	and again, I had to muster up all my strength to fight him.
MARIA:	I'm so sorry you had to go through that.
SABIR:	Hey, I'm here now. And anyway, what doesn't kill you makes you stronger, no?
ZARA:	Absolutely! Okay so what happened next?
SABIR:	So, we wrestled and wrangled until I had him pinned. And that's when he started to make these weird noises.
ZARA:	Noises? Because you were hurting him?
SABIR:	Not exactly. They sounded like calls. To his companions. Like a secret coded noise.
ZARA:	Whoa. So, what did you do?
SABIR:	I tried putting my hands over his mouth but he bit me. So, I-

(SABIR went quiet)

MARIA: It's okay grandad, you don't have to.

ZARA: Don't have to what?

SABIR: No, it's alright. I need to finish this.

ZARA: What is it grandad? What did you do?

SABIR: (sighs) I panicked. I had to survive and stop him making those sounds. So, I pulled out one of his eyes. That's what I see in my nightmares. Sometimes I'm running, sometimes I have an eyeball in front of me.

ZARA: (shocked) Oh grandad, I'm so sorry. I'm so sorry you went through all that. Did…did he die?

SABIR: He was still screaming when I ran from him, but I didn't look back. (He pauses) Wait, let me show you something.

(SABIR stood up and walked over to his chest of drawers, DSR. He opened the very last drawer and took out a brown paper bag. He took it over to the girls)

MARIA: (pointing at the bag) Is that what I think it is?

ZARA: What is it?

MARIA: I had heard of it but I never actually got to see it. If I'm correct, I think it's the clothes grandad was wearing that same night.

SABIR: That's right, I still have them.

ZARA: What? No way! That is amazing!

(MARIA gives ZARA a nudge)

ZARA: Sorry, I mean it is fascinating though.

(SABIR opens up the bag and takes out the stained salwar kameez)

ZARA: Whoa, is that…?

SABIR: Blood? Yes. Mine and his.

ZARA: This makes me so angry. Did you ever find out who it was?

SABIR: I have an idea, yes.

ZARA: Oh my God, who?

SABIR: No Zara. I'm not saying. There is no point in starting a feud, you know what your uncles are like. So this information will be going to the grave with me.

ZARA: Grandad! We can tell the police and get them arrested!

SABIR: Zara, I said no. Now please leave it.

(SABIR starts to get uncomfortable. MARIA nudges ZARA and gives her a funny look)

ZARA: Can I ask then, why have you kept the clothes after all these years?

SABIR: (wipes away a tear) So that I don't lose faith in Allah and to remind me that it was only prayer helped me through that

	night. This is a reminder of strong faith for me.
MARIA:	(smiling, holding back tears) That is amazing.
SABIR:	I love you both.
MARIA:	(holding ZARA'S hand) We love you too grandad.

The sun began to rise. Light was shining through an opening in the curtain, SR.

SABIR:	(smiling) Come on. It's time for morning prayer girls.

Acknowledgments

I would like to express my special thanks of gratitude to my family and friends for supporting me and believing in me. To my husband, Faisal, for having faith in me and for pushing me to do my absolute best. Faisal, you are my rock in this life and I thank God for you every day.

To my mother, my grandmother and my aunties – for raising me and teaching me to become the fierce woman I am today.

To my friend Natalie, for being an inspiration to women everywhere and for helping me believe in myself. Thank you, once again,

Irram Amin

Printed in Great Britain
by Amazon